Atchoo!
How We Catch a Cold

Leon Read
ILLUSTRATED BY **Sean Sims**

FRANKLIN WATTS
LONDON • SYDNEY

Franklin Watts

First published in
Great Britain in 2016 by
The Watts Publishing Group

Credits

Executive Editor: Adrian Cole
Design Manager: Peter Scoulding
Series Consultant: Jackie Hamley
Cover Designer: Cathryn Gilbert
Illustrations: Sean Sims

KIDWOW

Franklin Watts
An imprint of
Hachette Children's Group
Part of The Watts Publishing Group
Carmelite House, 50 Victoria Embankment
London EC4Y 0DZ

An Hachette UK Company
www.hachette.co.uk

www.franklinwatts.co.uk

HB ISBN:
978 1 4451 4625 6

Printed in China

When you catch a cold it usually means a virus is affecting your nose and throat. A sneeze helps to clear the nose and extra mucus washes it out.

HOLD ME UP TO THE LIGHT

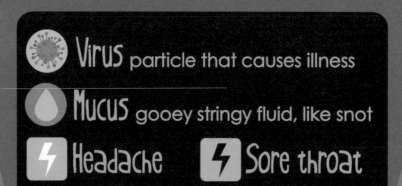

Square Bear Data File

Viruses that cause colds and other illnesses can survive for a short time in different places. They can be moved from one person to another.

Food and drink

Things we touch, like door handles

Shaking or touching hands

Using a dirty tissue

Kissing

19

Zap!

Zap!

Zap!

No, Jiffy, something better than lasers. Special cells that are in blood. Look at this.

HOLD ME UP TO THE LIGHT

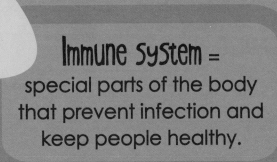

Immune System = special parts of the body that prevent infection and keep people healthy.

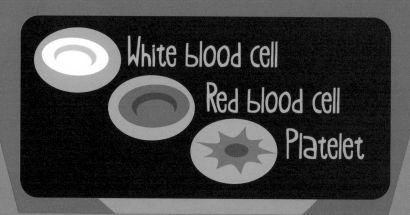

White blood cell
Red blood cell
Platelet

White blood cells are the body's soldiers. They help to fight against viruses and are part of the immune system.

Before modern medicines were discovered, people used other things to make themselves feel better. Can you guess which of these are still used today?

1 Egyptian mummy powder – for a headache

2 Mashed turnips – for a stuffy nose

3 Snail syrup – for a sore throat

4 Sweaty sock – for a cough

5 Lizard soup – for a sneeze

HOLD ME UP TO THE LIGHT

Change your pants every day.

Brush your teeth twice a day.

Have a regular bath or shower.

Catch a sneeze in a tissue.

Throw away used tissues.

Use soap to wash your hands before eating and after going to the toilet and playing outside or with animals.

Hygiene = things we can do to help us stay clean and healthy.

BEN'S ROOM

Only adults are allowed to give medicines. They have to be used in the right way.

Urgh! That medicine looks disgusting!

29

KiDWOW has been specially developed to provide an interactive way into human science for early readers.

Atchoo! How We Catch A Cold
This story explores some of the ways we can catch a viral cold, some of the basic symptoms, and simple ways to reduce infection. It aims to encourage children to have a developing awareness of their own body, but also the hidden world around them in a humorous and entertaining way.

WOW! look-through pages
These pages use the natural qualities of the wood-free paper to provide 'wow' moments for children as they interact in a different way with the book, enabling them to glimpse a world beyond their everyday experience.

HOW TO USE THIS BOOK
The book is designed for adults to share with either an individual child, or a group of children, and as a starting point for discussion.

The book also provides visual support, repeated words and phrases to build confidence in children who are starting to read on their own, in addition to key vocabulary.

Before reading this book
• Choose a time to read when you and the children are relaxed and have time to share the story.
• Look at the front and back cover – does anything catch their attention?
• Spend time looking at the illustrations inside, and talk about what the book may be about before reading it together.

After reading, talk about the book with the children:
• What was it about? Have the children ever caught a cold? What happened? Did they visit the doctor or pharmacist? What was the experience like?

• Talk about Ben's experiences in the story. Have the children had similar ones? Encourage them to use the names of parts of the body, such as throat, ears, chest when describing how they felt. Ask them to point to the parts as they name them. In a group, take the opportunity to promote good speaking and listening practice, such as speaking in turn and listening without interrupting.

• Talk about ways of keeping healthy in addition to personal hygiene, such as exercise and eating a balanced diet.

• Talk about medicines, and why only adults should administer them to help keep the children safe. When did they last have medicine? What are their experiences of tasting medicine?

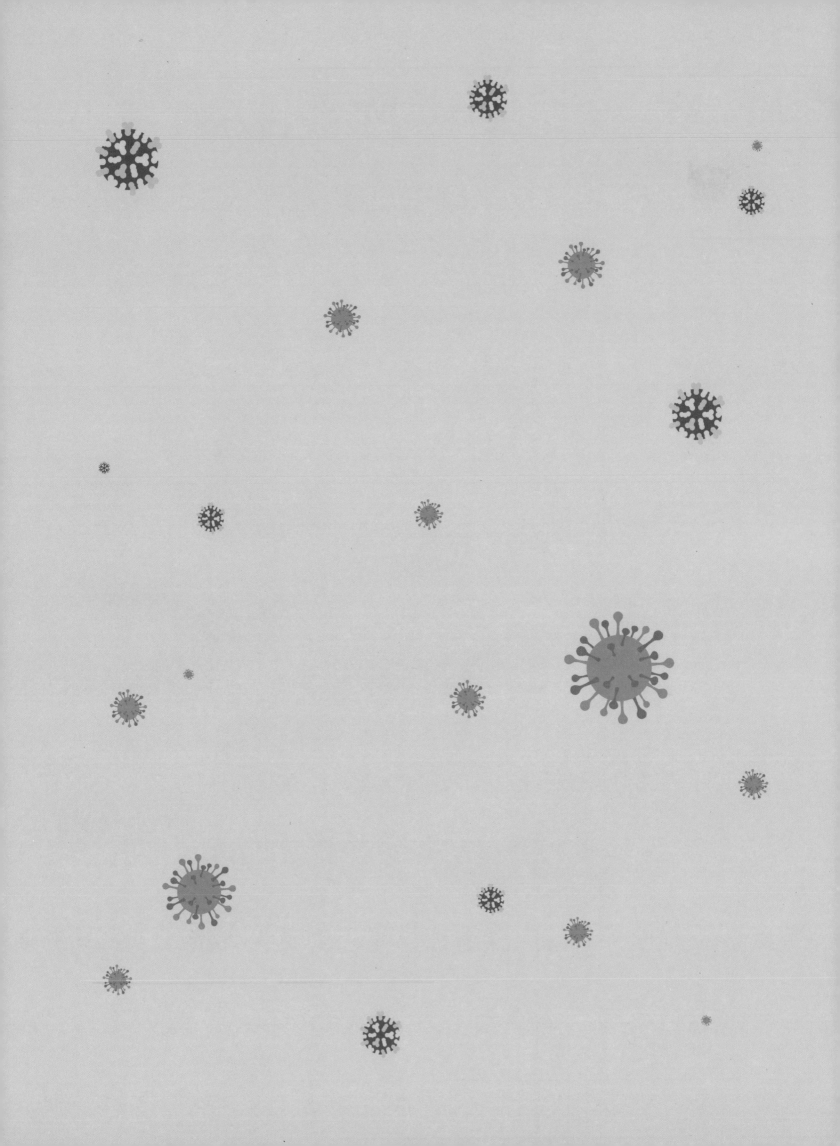